Rock Star

Rock Star

Adrian Chamberlain

orca soundings

ORCA BOOK PUBLISHERS

F I C
C H A

National Library of Canada Cataloguing in Publication Data

Chamberlain, Adrian, 1958-

Rock star / Adrian Chamberlain.

(Orca soundings)
ISBN 978-1-55469-236-1 (bound).--ISBN 978-1-55469-235-4 (pbk.)

I. Title. II. Series: Orca soundings

PS8605.H33R62 2010   jC813'.6   C2009-906848-6

First published in the United States, 2010
Library of Congress Control Number: 2009940839

Summary: When Duncan joins a rock band, he must decide if he is willing
to live the life and lose his friends, or make some tough decisions.

Orca Book Publishers gratefully acknowledges the support for its
publishing programs provided by the following agencies: the Government
of Canada through the Canada Book Fund and the Canada Council for the
Arts, and the Province of British Columbia through the BC Arts Council
and the Book Publishing Tax Credit.

Cover design by Teresa Bubela
Cover photography by iStockphoto

Orca Book Publishers   Orca Book Publishers
PO Box 5626, Stn. B   PO Box 468
Victoria, BC Canada   Custer, WA USA
V8R 6S4   98240-0468

www.orcabook.com
Printed and bound in Canada.
Printed on 100% PCW recycled paper.

13 12 11 10 • 4 3 2 1

For Penny and Katie

Chapter One

After school I walk up the front steps of our house and head straight for the kitchen. I'm starving. There's a peanut butter jar on the counter. But sure enough, someone's used it all up. Empty. That puts me in a bad mood.

There's almost nothing in the fridge. Some stuff that looks like dog food in a Tupperware container. Milk. Old celery.

I grab the celery and take a bite. Ugh. All wilty and squishy. So I bend over and gob it into the garbage bin. This is disgusting and weirdly satisfying at the same time.

I'm still bent over the garbage when Dad calls me into the living room.

"Duncan!" he yells. "Duncan!"

You'd think I was twelve or something, not fifteen. I'm in grade ten.

School's not my favorite thing, to tell you the truth. Mostly it's boring. Some days I even hate it.

But one thing I do like is the school band. I play bass guitar. Sure, the songs are pretty lame. What do you expect from a big orchestra, with clarinets and French horns and all that stuff? But playing bass guitar is pretty cool.

It's just me and Dad now. I don't have brothers and sisters or anything. Mom died two years ago. She had cancer. It was quick. One day she

sat down with me to tell me. She'd
been sick for a while, and the doctors
thought it was something else at first.
I forget what. But then they figured
out it was cancer. Six weeks later, she
was dead.

"Duncan McCann! Can you come in
here for a second?"

I stop gagging and stand there,
motionless, like a video on pause.
I thought the house was empty.
Something in Dad's voice sounds
different. I remain still. I've got a pretty
good imagination. If I pretend something, I can even forget what I was
doing before. Five seconds go by. Then
I walk into the living room. There's this
blond lady sitting on the couch with
Dad. Weird. Unbelievable. And Dad
looks kind of nervous or something.
Even though he's smiling.

"Duncan, I'd like to introduce you to
Terry. She's a friend of mine," says Dad.

"Hey, Duncan," the lady says. She's smiling. She's taller than Mom was. And sort of all-right-looking for an older lady. Dad's fifty. And Terry's probably forty or something. She's wearing a leather jacket. Mom would never have worn a leather jacket. Not in a million years.

"Hi," I say. I'm still holding my backpack. I drop it on the wood floor. It weighs a ton and makes a loud noise, like a kick drum.

"Yes. So anyway, Duncan. You'll be seeing a bit of Terry around the house. I mean, we're…well, seeing each other. She and I."

I was getting it now. Dad has a girlfriend. This lady. She smiles and holds out her hand.

"Okay," I say, shaking her hand. Then I pick up my pack and run upstairs to my room. I slam the door. I fall on my bed, face into my pillow, which sort of smells like corn chips. I'm not crying. I mean, I'm fifteen years old now. I'm not crying, but I feel like it.

After a while, I turn over. My face is still hot, but I feel better. I look around and—this may sound dumb—but I pretend I'm all alone on a desert island. Like I'm washed up on the beach, waking up with the tropical sun beating on my back. Then I look up. The walls of my room are mostly covered with posters of bands. I'm crazy about music. There's one of Death Cab for Cutie. An old Beastie Boys poster.

There's also a painting on the wall that my mom made. It's of a cabin by Shawnigan Lake. We once rented it for two weeks one summer. I was ten. That was my best summer. We swam in the lake almost every day. When I dived down, I could see green shafts of sunlight underwater. After swimming, me and my friend Jason would go to the corner store to buy candy. We walked in the dirt beside the road. Brown powdery dust squished up between my toes. Sounds dumb now, but back then I thought that was the greatest.

I've got Mom's beat-up old record player on my desk. I've got all her records too. She liked the Beatles a lot. I put on her favorite song. It's called "Here, There and Everywhere." It's a sappy ballad, but I like it. I think about Dad and this Terry lady, then about Mom. And then—I'm embarrassed to admit it—I start crying. For real. Blubbering all over the place. What a loser.

My cell phone buzzes. It's Jason's number. I don't answer. I don't feel like talking. Instead, I go back to pretending I'm on that desert island. I'm facedown on the bed, pretending my ship has gone down. It's late morning, and the sun's killing my back. Pretty soon I've gotta get up and build my shelter. Maybe find some food. Like turtle eggs. I read once how some guy on a desert island had to eat turtle eggs. Would that be like chicken eggs? Probably not.

I roll over, kind of slip-sliding off my bed onto the floor. Then I get my bass guitar out of the closet. Put the record-player needle back to the beginning of "Here, There and Everywhere" and start to play along. It sounds all right. I got my bass about a year ago. Actually, Dad bought it for me. But for a long time I didn't feel like learning to play it. I was pretty depressed. I even had to go to a psychiatrist for a while. Dad was worried about me because I got real sad after Mom died. For a while, I didn't want to get out of bed. Maybe for, like, two weeks. After that, Dad made me go to that stupid shrink.

After "Here, There and Everywhere," I try to play along with some other songs on the Beatles record. But it doesn't sound as good. Then I hear Dad yelling from downstairs for me to set the table. That's one of my jobs. Also, I clean one of the bathrooms every weekend, take out the garbage and sometimes help Dad make dinner.

Terry has gone home, so it's just me and Dad at dinner.

"Duncan," he says, dabbing his lips with a napkin. "Did you know Terry is a bank teller?"

"Nope," I say.

"Yes. She's quite an interesting lady. We were, you know, talking about films. Movies. And her favorites are…let me remember. Oh yes. *When Harry Met Sally*. And that other one, you know, about that large ship that hits an iceberg."

"*Titanic*," I say. I cram some peas into my mouth. How can Dad not know that?

He goes on to tell me that Terry lives in Esquimalt, which is part of Victoria, where we live. I don't ask Dad one thing about Terry. I'm kind of mad or confused or something, which is actually how I feel a lot of the time. It's like my emotions boil up and it's hard to control them. Weird, I know.

I help do the dishes after supper. Dad talks a lot about some guys at his work, and who said what to who and what so-and-so thought about so-and-so. It sounds mean, but I wish he'd shut up, because it's incredibly boring. But I don't want to hurt his feelings, so I just dry the dishes and say nothing.

I go back up to my room, leaving Dad to watch some dumb TV show. Something about monkeys. Dad is crazy about nature shows. If there's a monkey or a giraffe or a lion or a koala bear on TV, he has to watch it. I like action movies—like James Bond movies or *Collateral*—or shows about police detectives trying to solve old murders. Cold cases, they're called. I like it best when they dig up an old skull or hold up the rusty, crappy old hammer some maniac used to kill some poor guy, or when they look at a bloodstained pillowcase under a microscope. I guess that's sort of weird. But I make no apologies.

I put the Beatles record back on and play along to "Here, There and Everywhere" again. Then I get under my covers, not even taking my clothes off. I shut my eyes, sniff my smelly old corn-chip pillow and pretend I'm on that desert island again, thinking about those turtle eggs. They'd be all mushy inside, right? But, hey, you gotta eat to survive.

After a while my thoughts get all confused. You know how it is just before you fall asleep, and your mind starts to go into free fall, where anything goes?

From the desert island I go back to that summer at Shawnigan Lake, swimming in the green water with sunlight shafting into the deeper brown-black water. Some big dark fish are down below— it's scary for some reason. And then I'm dreaming…dreaming that I'm sinking deeper and deeper, and that I can still see the sunlight. But it's far, far above. And then I'm asleep.

Chapter Two

The next day at school, I plop myself down at my usual lunch table. Fake wood grain, bright orange plastic chairs. I always sit with the same people—guys I've known since elementary school. It's kind of boring in a way. Then again, it's nice to have somewhere to sit where you belong.

Our lunchroom is big on cliques. The cool kids always hang out with the cool kids, the smart kids sit with the smart kids, the jocks sit with the other jocks. What's my table like? Well, I hate to admit it…but we might be a nerd table.

Most of my friends are into stuff like video games, science fiction books, *Star Wars*, *Star Trek*—even the old-school *Star Trek* shows from the 1960s. Things like that.

I used to be into all that stuff too. I really liked the old-school *Star Trek*. I could talk for hours about the Vulcans and Spock and all. My best friend Jason and I have this joke—if you can call it a joke. We'd always point a finger at each other and yell, "Warp drive!" Warp drive means the faster-than-light way the *Star Trek* spaceship travels through space after nuclear war destroyed planet Earth. I don't know why we would say something so stupid and uncool to each other. I guess we thought it was funny.

Jason and I look totally different. I've got dark hair, almost black. Jason's got red hair. He also has tons of freckles and wears gold wire-rimmed glasses. He's always joking around, and he's always in a good mood. Not like me. I guess that's why we're best friends.

"Warp drive!" says Jason, pointing his finger at me as I sit down. I just grunt. Jason's getting every single thing out of his lunch bag and arranging it on the table, like he always does. He's a precise sort of guy. His mom, who's really nice, always makes him a good lunch. Sandwiches wrapped in wax paper, apple, granola bar, home-baked cake. The works. I make my own lunch now. Today it's two Pizza Pops. That's it. Pretty crappy, but I'm too lazy to make anything good.

Most of our friends are really into computers. Not just computer games. They actually know tons about computers, like how to fix them and program them and all. Have you ever noticed that these kinds of guys usually dress horribly? They look like their mom dressed them. Which might even be true. Donnie, sitting next to Jason, wears a little striped Charlie Brown T-shirt, like a six-year-old would wear. Steve's got a short-sleeved sport shirt, buttoned up to his neck.

They're all talking loudly about some big stupid computer project they're working on. Steve's so excited, a bit of the sandwich he's eating dribbles down the side of his chin. Leaks right down.

"Steve, for Christ's sake!" I say.

He looks over.

"What?"

"Steve. Steve-o. Your chin," says Jason. He points to his own chin. Steve rubs the sandwich guck off with the back of his hand.

"Can't take these guys anywhere," says Jason.

I bite into my Pizza Pop. Then something embarrassing happens. Something really terrible. The Pizza Pop explodes, just like in the TV commercial. A bunch of the red stuff inside, like tomato paste, squirts out about three feet onto the floor beside me. A couple of girls at the next table look over and giggle.

I can feel my face getting red and hot.

"Hey, Dunc! Like a zit," says Steve.

"Yeah. Pop that zit," Donnie says, laughing like a maniac.

"Shut up, you dildos," I say. "Grow up."

I look around, but by now no one at the other tables is looking. It's always busy in the cafeteria at lunch. Lots of talking, echoing noise. Bright fluorescent lights. I don't like it here much, if you want to know the truth.

Jason looks around, then looks at me for a second. Then he says, "Hey, how did you do on McGregor's test?"

Mr. McGregor is our social studies teacher. This morning we got our midterm tests back. The test was mostly on Europe, like what are the capitals of Europe and the special features of each city. You know, like how the Eiffel Tower is a special feature of Paris. Also some history stuff.

Socials used to be one of my best subjects. But this term, I've got to admit, I haven't actually done much work. I barely studied for the test. So, as a result, my test mark is quite lame.

"D," I say.

"What?"

"D. Well…D plus."

"Jesus." Jason looks at me again. "Jesus, Duncan. That's pretty bad."

"Yeah, I know. I don't need you to tell me that."

"Your dad's gonna kill you."

I hadn't thought about that. Dad's going to be mad, that's for sure. He always puts a lot of stock in school grades. Mom did too. But for some reason, this year I don't feel like studying so much. I used to be a really good student. Mostly Bs. Sometimes an A, like in band or art.

Jason doesn't say anything about his own test mark. I bet you he aced it though. Jason is a very smart guy. He gets mostly As. But he doesn't brag. He hardly ever talks about how well he does in school. And if you ever need help on a math problem or whatever, he'll always help you. Jason is a pretty good guy, all right.

"Hey," he says, "have you talked to that girl yet?"

"What girl?" I say. But I know exactly who he's talking about. Exactly.

There's this girl in band that I like. Jennifer. She plays clarinet. She's pretty, with long brown hair. Everyone likes Jennifer. But she's not one of those stuck-up good-looking girls. She's nice. At least, I think she is. I haven't exactly worked up the courage to talk to her yet. Any conversation we've had has been in my imagination. Or, as Dad would say, my overactive imagination. But I've looked at her quite a few times, whenever I get the chance.

Mostly I just see the back of her head though. That's because the bass guitar player—that is, me—always gets stuck way at the back of the band, beside the drums. I sit beside the guy who plays the big bass drum. He's a good guy, but he's also sort of a dumbass. I guess you don't have to be a rocket scientist to play the bass drum. And—I hate to say it—he farts all the time. Which is not cool at all in my book.

"What girl? I'm talking about Jennifer. From band," says Jason.

"Nope," I say, biting into my second Pizza Pop, but carefully this time, just in case. "No talkee. Not so far."

"Well, you should."

"I know that. Tell me something I don't know."

Jason keeps quiet for a second. I can see he's working himself up to something. Something different. That's because I've known him since we were in grade two. When he has something important to say, his face goes all blank, then he sort of squints his left eye. It's a total giveaway.

"Hey, Dunc. I did something. I did something for you. On your behalf.

But don't get pissed off now," he says. "Okay?"

I hesitate for a second, then say, "What?"

Jason's quiet. Then he says, "I answered that ad. In the school newspaper. You know the one. That ad."

He meant an ad we had noticed in the school paper for a bass player. Jason kept encouraging me to answer it. But I wasn't so sure. It said *Wanted: Bass player for totally kick-ass rock band. No newbies or dweebs need apply.*

Jason says, "I knew you wanted to do it. You know, play in a band and everything. So I emailed the guy. It's Grant Newson. See over there?" He points a couple of tables away.

Grant Newson. He's like Mr. Rock and Roll at our school. He always wears a leather jacket—one that's all beat-up and rugged-looking. He used to be a total jock, on the basketball team and the football team. But now he just plays guitar and sings in rock bands. The girls are all crazy about him.

"Jason. Jay. J-man. You shouldn't have done that." I'm a little pissed.

"I know. But it's all good. I emailed him. I pretended I was you. He said he wants to meet you."

I look over at Grant. He's got one of his rocker friends in a headlock a few tables down. Grant's laughing like crazy. The girls at the next table are laughing too. Not at him. But laughing like they think Grant's cool and all.

"Jesus," I say.

For the next five minutes, Jason lists all the reasons why I should walk over and introduce myself. Mostly, it's all about how I like music and would love to be in a band. It's true. I'd really, really like to be in a rock band. Plus, you can only play bass guitar in the dorky school orchestra for so long.

But I feel nervous and just plain scared about walking over to Grant—Mr. Popularity, Mr. Rock and Roll. I hate to say it, but I'm not that popular. I'm pretty shy. I don't feel cool enough to just walk over.

It's a funny thing, but sometimes I feel okay about myself. And sometimes I wonder if I'm some kind of freak. I mean, if you're a weirdo, you probably don't realize it, right? Otherwise, why would you act like that? Nobody says to himself, "Hey…I want to be really weird in my day-to-day life." For weird people, weirdness is normal.

So what if I'm weird and everyone knows it except me? And it's the kind of thing no one will explain to you. Like, no one's going to say, "Hey, Duncan, I don't know if you realize it, but you are a weirdo and, in fact, some kind of total freak." You ever feel like that? Maybe it's just me. Maybe I *am* a freak.

Plus, my clothing choice today isn't so good. In fact, it's pretty bad. I'm wearing these old jeans that are way too small for me. They're like flood pants, about two inches too short. And I'm wearing an Oak Bay High T-shirt that seemed like a good idea when I bought it, but turned out to be way too tight after my dad washed it. So basically I look like a dorky little kid in these retarded, miniature clothes.

"Just walk over," says Jason. "Come on. Go."

I actually want to. I really do. So I make myself get up and walk toward Grant's table. That's not like me. It feels like I'm in a dream or something. Like it's not really me. Like I'm floating.

About halfway over, I trip, hitting my knees and hands hard. I get up, my face is burning. I can hear people laughing, lots of people. Everything's in slow motion. All my senses are on red alert.

I can smell tuna sandwich and greasy French fries. Someone must have tripped me. I look over, and sure enough there's this fat dude in a rugby shirt with a big fat face, laughing at me. His leg's still sticking out. He's pointing to it, laughing like a hyena.

I don't know why—I've never done this before—but I swing at the guy. Crazy. I connect too, hitting the side of his jumbo pumpkin noggin. Things are happening fast now. He punches me right in the mouth, then lands another on my forehead. I try to slug the guy again, but just then someone pins my arms behind me. Mr. McGregor. Ow.

"Break it up, McCann," he says.

"But he tripped me!"

"Break it up. Both of you. I mean it. Or I'll send you to the principal's office. Now."

The guy in the rugby shirt stops short for a second. Then he shakes his head, laughs and goes back to talking to his buddies. Just like nothing happened.

For some reason, maybe because I'm already halfway there, I walk the rest of the way to the Grant's table. Even though I'm embarrassed and feeling weird and beat-up and like a total freak. Everyone at the table is looking at me like something funny's going on. Which I guess it is.

"Hey," I say.

Nobody says anything.

"Hey," I say again, but louder. I feel like I'm on stage.

Grant looks at me. His face is blank.

"Hey there, fighter dude. Nice bruise on your forehead. Who're you?" he says.

"Um. I'm Duncan. Duncan McCann."

Grant says nothing. It's uncomfortable. One of his buddies snorts, then makes this farting noise.

"I'm the bass player…who answered the ad." My voice sounds small and all wimpy. This happens sometimes when I get nervous.

"Oh yeah?" says Grant.

"Not McCann. He's a goof," says Grant's buddy. With his crew cut and thick neck, he looks like a weight lifter. He looks like an extra-large bulldog. Kind of like the guy who tripped me, actually.

"Shut up," says Grant to the bulldog. Then he turns back to me. "Can you play?"

"Yeah," I say.

"McCann doesn't know how to play bass," says Bulldog.

"Hey, didn't I tell you to shut up?" says Grant. He's still looking at me, like he's sizing me up or something.

"Can you come to our jam tomorrow after school?" he says.

"Uh, yeah. No problem."

"Okay." Grant writes his address out on a piece of paper. He tells me to be there at 4:00. Then he turns back to his buddies again. I walk back to our table. My face is on fire, like a bad sunburn.

"So," says Jason. "I can't believe that guy who tripped you."

"Yeah."

"What happened? With Newson, I mean."

"I'm gonna try out," I say. "You know, like an audition."

"Cool."

"Yeah," I say. I feel all nervous and jumbled up inside. But happy too. In fact, I'm excited like I haven't been for a long time. Ever since before Mom died, anyway.

Chapter Three

I wake up thinking, *Oh man. Not another day of school.* Then I remember the rock band audition with Grant Newson. The bottom of my stomach gets all tingly.

Of course, I've got to make sure I don't forget to bring my bass to school. That would be a disaster. Besides, I need it for my band class. That's the first class of the day, in fact.

I'm almost late for school because I have to lug my amp as well as my guitar. Plus I've got my usual jumbo backpack of books along for the ride. Band class goes okay, although the dude who plays bass drum is farting like crazy, of course. What does this guy eat for breakfast? Because it's not working out for him.

After we play a medley of Disney movie tunes for forty-five minutes—why Disney, for the love of god?—class is over. I see Jennifer, the girl I kind of like. She looks over at me and actually smiles. Wow. So I make myself walk over. Heck, if I can do it with Grant Newson, I can do it with her, right?

"Hi," I say.

"Hi there. You're Duncan, right?"

"Yeah...Hey, I like the way you play clarinet."

"You can really hear me?" she says. "From all the way at the back?" She smiles. This Jennifer is a really cool girl.

"Well, not really. But you, uh...look like you're having fun playing your horn and all."

Jennifer smiles again, almost laughing. Then she closes her clarinet case.

"Well...," she says, "see you next band class, I guess."

Crap. Having fun playing your horn? Why did I say something so stupid? Is a clarinet even a horn? I don't know. What an idiot.

The rest of the day is a drag. Even more than usual. That's because I'm waiting for 4:00 to roll around. The teachers just drone on and on.

History. English. Math. The day takes forever.

Finally the bell rings. I've got to phone a cab to get to Grant's house, which makes me sort of uptight. Plus I have to drag my bass amp along. But Dad gave me the money for a taxi, so it's cool. I kill time until 3:30 PM, just sitting on the front lawn of the school, then phone for the cab.

"Here's the place," says the cab driver, pulling up. Man. It's kind of a dump. I'm not a snob or anything. I mean, our house isn't exactly a mansion. But this place looks like it needed a new coat of paint in 1971.

A note on the front door says *McCann: Go around to the side of the house. Basement door*. Well, at least Grant remembered my name. That's a good sign.

Now I can hear the guys playing... it's really loud. I knock and knock and knock. There's quiet. Birds are chirping. Then Grant opens the door.

"Hey, man," he says.

"Uh…hey," I say.

I'm trying to act cool, but I am really nervous. The other guys in the band don't even say hi or anything. They all have long hair to their shoulders. Some are wearing jean jackets with the names of heavy-metal bands written in ink.

"That your amp?" says Grant, pointing.

"Yeah."

"That's not gonna work here. Too small. You better plug into that one."

The other guys laugh at my tiny amp. So I plug into this huge black monster. It's all battered, like it's been on the road with Metallica for twenty years. I'm sort of freaking out, to tell the truth.

"Okay. You know 'Death to the Enemy'?" says Grant.

"Um. No."

"Well, just try to follow along."

The drummer counts it off, and then the band starts playing this really fast song. Loud? It's like being at an airport when a jet takes off. Grant is singing—actually, it's more like screaming—and playing guitar.

For the first verse I don't know what I'm doing. Just faking it. For starters, it's so loud it kind of throws me off. It's like someone's hitting my head with a baseball bat. Then after a while I start to figure it out, just like I work out the Beatles songs on Mom's old record player. There's a pattern to follow that keeps coming around.

The drummer does a big, flashy ending, hitting practically every drum and cymbal on his kit. And it's a honking big kit.

"That was okay," says Grant. "Seems like you caught on after a while."

"Yeah, after a while," says the drummer. He's a really tall guy, unshaven. He looks about twenty. I can tell he's not my biggest fan.

The audition lasts an hour. Basically, Grant calls out tunes, the drummer counts in and we blast it out. Or at least, they do. I'm just trying to catch up, like a water-skier trying not to fall.

Then it's over. Everybody's packing up. No one says anything to me, so I figure I was pretty horrible and will now slink off in total disgrace. I'm surprised that when I leave, Grant follows me outside.

"We practice once a week. Every Wednesday at four. The band's called Primal Thunk, by the way."

"Huh? You mean…I'm in?"

"Oh yeah. Guess so. You're not the greatest bass player, McCann. But then again, you're the only one who answered the ad," says Grant. He's grinning though.

"Wow. Thanks!"

"But you're gonna have to grow out your hair. You don't look metal enough."

"Okay."

"And buy some better clothes," he says. "Jean jacket, or leather or something. You sort of look like a dork in that outfit."

I don't even mind that Grant called me a dork, although that's usually the kind of comment that makes me mad. I'm so happy, I don't even phone a cab to get home. It's not that far, anyway. I can walk—you know, burn off my energy. And I have lots of energy now. I'm in a heavy-metal band! Unbelievable. How cool is that? Pri-mal Thunk, Pri-mal Thunk. And on bass…Duncan McCann! Yeah! Welcome to my life as a rock star. I'm grinning from ear to ear, no doubt looking like a total goob as I walk along lugging my bass in one hand and my weeny amp in the other.

At home Dad asks me how it went. I tell him it was good, even give him a hug (he looks surprised), then run upstairs to my room. I get a call from Jason.

"How'd it go?" he says right off.

"Good, man," I say.

"Well?"

"I'm in the band. It's called Primal Thunk."

"Hey, that's so cool!" Jason says.

"Yeah."

"Maybe if you guys record your music, we can use it for the movie."

I don't say anything for a second. Jason's talking about this thing we've been working on since grade seven. It's kind of embarrassing. I don't talk about it. It's our version of *Raiders of the Lost Ark*. We're doing it ourselves, with an old video camera Jason's mom gave him.

Jason plays Indiana Jones, wearing a fedora hat and all. I play all the other characters because I'm good at doing different voices and stuff. The problem is, we're three years older now than at the beginning of the movie. So at the start it looks like Harrison Ford's a little kid. It's a stupid movie. But Jason's really stoked on doing it, and I don't have the heart to tell him I've lost interest.

"Duncan?"

"Yeah. I'm still here. I don't know, Jason. We'll have to see. I mean, I just joined the band."

"Sure, sure. No problem. Keep it in mind though."

After dinner, I pull out a mix CD that Grant has given me and shove it in my player. It has all the songs that the band does. About nine in all. The music is pretty hard. It's so fast, and it changes all the time. After about half an hour, I get discouraged. I unplug my guitar and just lie back on my bed. It's been a pretty long day. But all in all, one of my better ones, I've got to admit.

Chapter Four

The next day everything goes wrong. First of all, I'm still ignoring my homework, and I'm catching hell in every one of my classes.

Biology. Forgot to do my homework. Mrs. Meyers bawls me out in front of the whole class. Then math. Pop quiz. I know I blew that one. Then English. Another test that I forgot to study for. Man, I didn't even read the book it was all about. Probably lost it, in fact.

When I get home, I slam the wooden screen door. All I want to do is go to my room and practice my Primal Thunk tunes. But then Dad calls me.

"Duncan? Can you come in here for a minute?"

So I walk into the living room. Dad's sitting on the couch with Terry.

"Duncan, I have to run out now. I forgot something at the office. So can you keep Terry company? I should only be an hour."

Dad leaves. This all seems a little fishy to me. An hour? Jesus. I plop myself into the easy chair across from Terry. What a day. First I'm screwing up at school. Now this.

"So, how were your classes today, Duncan?" says Terry.

"Okay, I guess."

I don't feel like talking. Especially to Terry. She's trying hard, all cheerful, asking about school and what kind of movies I like. I'm giving two-word answers. I'm being kind of a dork, I guess. But why did Dad leave me with his stupid girlfriend anyhow?

The radio's on in the kitchen. It's the CBC, which is Dad's favorite. I never listen to it because it's so boring. But then this really cool song comes on. There's no singing or anything. It has this really great keyboard riff. Really grungy sounding. Grinding, you know? And at the end of each riff, an electric guitar snaps, really hard, like a whip.

Terry's talking about something, but I'm not listening. I'm tuned into that song on the radio.

"That's 'Green Onions,'" she says.

"What?" I'd almost forgotten about Terry. It was like I was dreaming.

"The song on the radio. That's what it is."

"Oh," I say. "Sorry. I was… distracted."

"That's okay," said Terry. She smiles. "You sure like music a lot, huh?"

"Yeah. I guess. That's a good song."

"It's by Booker T. and the MG's."

Man, you could have knocked me over with a PEZ dispenser. I didn't know Terry knew anything about music. I mean, Dad knows zip. Even Mom didn't know that much, aside from liking the Beatles. Maybe Terry is cooler than I thought.

"Really?" I say. "That one crunchy riff they play? I really like that."

"You mean the organ? That's a Hammond B-3 organ. That's what Booker T. plays."

"An organ? You mean like a church organ?"

"Well, yeah. They used them in churches," says Terry. "But all the old soul bands used Hammond organs too. They're the best."

"Sounds great. All raspy."

"That's because the organ's over-driving the speaker. Those speakers have tubes in them. Too much input, and they get that great grinding sound."

I thought about that for a second.

"Soul music? What's that?"

"It's like rhythm-and-blues music," says Terry. "You know—Otis Redding, James Brown, Aretha Franklin. All soul singers."

"Soul singers. Hey, how come you know all this stuff?"

Terry laughs. When she smiles, the corners of her eyes go all crinkly.

"My brother, Houston. He's a professional musician. Or was. He's a Hammond B-3 player."

Holy crap. This Terry is way cooler than I thought. The sister of a real musician. How about that? Then she starts asking me about my music, about playing the bass. Unbelievable. Dad never asks me about that stuff. Never. I tell her what kind of music I like and all about the heavy-metal band. I'm talking way more than normal, like I do when I get excited about something. I tell her about walking over to Grant Newson in the cafeteria and the fight. I even told her about Mom and the Beatles records.

Then Terry starts talking about her brother, Houston. He used to be in a lot of soul bands. One of them, The Amazing Rhythm Kings, used to play clubs all the time and even got their music played on the radio. They opened a few times for some big bands at the Royal Theatre, which is a famous theatre in Victoria.

"Hey, maybe I can go see his band sometime?" I say.

"Well…no. He's not playing in a band anymore," says Terry.

"How come?"

"Well…Houston has some problems. I think the stress got to him. He used to run everything. You know, booking the band, producing their CDs, running the rehearsals, driving the van. It got to be too much."

Terry looks away for a second. I think maybe she's choked up or something. But I can't tell, not knowing her that well. Plus, with older people I never know what's going on.

"Oh. That's too bad," I say.

"Yeah. Well. Maybe you'd like to meet him sometime. Houston would like that."

That sounded okay. Then something funny happens. It sounds weird, but I suddenly figure Terry is being too friendly or something. Like maybe she's trying to be my mom. You know, take the place of my mom? Sounds crazy. But that's what I feel like.

There's a crunching sound in the driveway. It's Dad pulling up. Got back early, I guess.

"I better go up and do some home-work now," I say.

"Okay. Bye," says Terry.

"Yeah."

I run upstairs and toss my back-pack of books into the corner. Bad aim. The bag slams the bottom of my bass, which is leaning in the corner. It falls over with a kind of *ker-plang* noise, like a cartoon. I swear softly and grab my bass. It's okay. Thank god, because I have no money for repairs. Then I put on the Primal Thunk practice CD. I can hear Dad and Terry talking downstairs.

I can't make out the words. It sounds like "Babble, babble, babble." I turn my bass up a little, not too loud, and play along. It's starting to sound not too bad, if I do say so myself.

Soon I forget school. And I forget about talking with Terry. The only thing that matters right now—just this second—is hitting the right note. The next note, the one that's right in front of me.

Chapter Five

We're playing a concert at Victoria High School today. I don't mean Primal Thunk. I'm talking about the school orchestra with the corny Walt Disney tunes. And, worst of all, we're playing our so-called rock medley. Ever hear a school orchestra play tunes by ABBA, the Jonas Brothers and Britney Spears? Yeah. Case closed.

But it's okay. Because Jennifer's in the school band too.

The concert's in the school gym. Not that I care that much, because the music is quite lame, but the acoustics are really horrible. Everything echoes. And the kids from Vic High seem kind of bored by the whole thing. Hey, I would be too. They're sitting in the bleachers, kidding around. Our band teacher, Mr. Craigson, turns around and yells, "Please, would you give us the basic courtesy of keeping your chatter to a dull roar!"

I guess he thought he was being funny and all. It's weird that adults think they're being funny or cute, and they're so obviously not. It's like they come from a different country or something. The country of the uncool. It's like my dad, who used to call my skateboard a surfboard.

Anyway, the concert's finally over. I'm packing up my bass and pulling off my tie. Did I tell you we all have to wear ties and white shirts for the school orchestra shows? Another one of Craigson's brilliant ideas.

"Hey, Duncan." I look up. It's Jennifer.

"Hey," I say. "How's it going?"

We joke around a little about the concert and how the Vic High kids seemed bored and all. I'm getting better at feeling relaxed with Jennifer. This is good, because I'm usually not too cool around girls, if you want to know the truth.

"What are you going to do now?" she says.

"Oh, I'll probably hop the bus."

"My parents are going to pick me up in half an hour," Jennifer says. "Hey, do you want to grab a coffee? We could walk over to the coffee shop on the corner."

Man, does this ever make me happy. Jennifer wants to hang out with me.

I'm over the moon. So we walk over. I carry my bass and her clarinet case, even though she says she could manage it herself.

Jennifer's really easy to talk to. For one thing, she always seems to know the right thing to say. She says my bass playing is good, even though I think she's just being polite. For one thing, with the school orchestra, it's so loud it's almost impossible to hear any one player.

At the coffee shop, which is almost empty, Jennifer orders herbal tea. Jasmine. I have a Coke and tell her all about Primal Thunk. The whole story—even the part about walking over to Grant Newson that day in the cafeteria and getting into that fight. I haven't seen the guy I got into the scrap with again, by the way. Hope I never do.

I also tell Jennifer how Grant wants me to look more metal. You know, grow my hair and get some new clothes.

"They want you to change how you look to be in the band?" she asks.

"Yeah."

"Really? I like the way your hair is now," she says. "You know, short. Or shortish."

"Well. It's all about image, I guess." I shrug. "You know, if you're in a metal band you have to look the part."

"I guess," says Jennifer. "What do your mom and dad say?"

"My mom isn't around anymore."

"Oh. Sorry. Your parents are divorced?"

I didn't say anything for a second or two. I'm still not that comfortable talking about what happened to Mom.

"My mom passed away a couple of years ago. She had cancer."

"Oh. Duncan, I'm sorry."

"Yeah, well." I look out the window for a second. I can see a mom yelling at her kid. The kid's crying. Weird.

"Anyway, my dad probably wouldn't care that much if I had long hair and stuff. He's mostly interested in his new girlfriend."

I tell Jennifer all about Terry. The funny thing, though, is that while I'm talking, I realize I really do like Terry. It's cool she knows about music. As I talk, I make a mental note to take Terry up on her offer to visit her brother, the musician.

"So you're gonna buy some clothes? Like, for the band?" Jennifer says after sipping her tea.

"I guess. I don't know what to get though. I'm not that into fashion."

"I could help you shop. I love clothes shopping."

Jennifer looks kind of shy when she says that. Like she isn't sure how I'm going to react. I know how she feels. I'm always nervous when I ask someone new if they want to do stuff.

"Sure," I say. "That'd be great."

She smiles and stands up.

"I better go back to the school. My parents will be there in a few minutes."

I'm so happy, I feel like hugging Jennifer or something. But I just say goodbye. Then I sit by myself in the coffee shop for a while, drinking my Coke. Another good day. Imagine that.

I look through the window to see if that mom and her crying kid are still around. No sign of them. At that moment, sunlight shining through the window lights up my hands. Just my hands. I figure, for some crazy reason, that this is a good sign.

Chapter Six

Saturday morning. The weekend's finally here. I love sleeping in, especially on Saturdays. Sometimes the sun comes through the window and warms up my legs under the covers. I like to pretend I'm on that tropical island and doze off for another hour or two.

Then I look at the digital clock on the bedside table. It's 10:47 AM. Wow.

Some sleep. Still, instead of getting up, I yank the covers over my head. I start thinking about Jennifer.

I imagine that we're married, you know, husband and wife. We live in a white house with a white fence. Even our car is white. And there's these yellow daffodils planted all around the house. It's sort of like a cartoon, really, or one of those movies where everything is kind of fake on purpose. Like that neighborhood in *Edward Scissorhands*, where all the lawns are cut just right and the houses are bright colors.

"Duncan!" my dad yells. "Duncan! Come on down. Get some breakfast."

Breakfast? Dad never makes breakfast. Mom used to do that. Now we usually get our own stuff. Half the time I don't even eat breakfast.

I sniff. Pancakes. Pancakes and sausages. Unbelievable.

I'm just wearing a T-shirt and underwear. Briefs, not boxers. I can't believe people who wear boxers. Me, I need the support. When I walk in the kitchen, guess what? There's Terry, standing over the stove, cooking up pancakes and sausages. Holy crap.

"Hey, buster," she says. "Nice pajamas."

Dammit. Why doesn't Dad tell me his girlfriend's sleeping over? I mean, I guess she was. She's making breakfast, after all.

I run my hand through my hair and don't say anything. Instead, I just sit down at the breakfast table, kind of slumped down. I pick up a fork and just stare at it. If Terry wants to check me out in my underwear, she can be my guest.

Terry looks at me, looks like she's going to say something, but doesn't. Instead, she hands me a plate of sausages and pancakes. They look pretty good,

I have to admit. But am I going to give her the satisfaction of eating them? Nope. Who does Terry think she is, my mom?

Terry goes out of the room. Then I hear it. That song again, "Green Onions." The organ sounds so cool, so grindy, so…you know. Greasy, I guess. Greasier than these sausages, which I'm starting to eat by now. I'm listening to this song so hard, I forget to be mad at Terry anymore.

She sits across from me at the table, not saying anything. Terry looks ready to smile, but like she's trying to hold it in or something.

"Man…," I say, my mouth full of sausages and pancake. "I love that song!" But it comes out like "Mo.. Isa orf ack long." Because of the sausages and all.

Terry laughs. She's got a pretty good laugh. It sounds kind of cackly and crackly. But in a good way, not a Wicked Witch of the West way.

"I bought you an album. It's called the *Best of Classic Soul*. Here."

She hands over the CD case. There's "Green Onions" by Booker T. and the MG's. Lots of different guys. Ray Charles singing "What I Say." "Hold On" by Sam and Dave.

The next song comes on. It's a lady singing, "What you want...baby, I got. What you need...you know I got it. All I'm asking...is for a little respect." It sounds cool. She's got a great, big-beltin' voice. No nonsense, no foolin' around. And those rhythms, they're so great. I start to tap the tabletop with my hand. Can't help it.

"That's Aretha Franklin," Terry says. "Wonderful singer. The best. Queen of Soul."

Dad comes in. He's smiling and looks happy.

"Hi, you two. What's up?"

"We're just listening to the album," says Terry.

"Really," says Dad. "You like it, Duncan?"

"Yeah," I say. "It's okay, I guess."

I kind of hate it when grown-ups ask you if you like something. If they ask that, they *want* you to like it. You sort of have no choice. It makes me feel like saying I hate whatever it is. Don't ask me why. But it does.

Still, it was cool of Terry to buy me that album. After breakfast, I go to my room to practice Primal Thunk's songs some more. After that, I have to get through the huge list of jobs Dad's left for me. All written on a piece of notepad, just like Mom used to. Like mowing the lawn and helping him fix part of the backyard balcony that's rotted away. There's also cleaning up my room, which, I admit, really needs it.

For starters, I found three dried-up apple cores under the bed. Not to mention an old cheese sandwich that was partly green. Gross.

There's a Primal Thunk practice at 4:00 PM today. I'm going to wear my new clothes. My rocker duds. Jennifer helped me pick them out at Mayfair Mall. Actually, it's just one thing—a jean jacket. It's a pre-faded one that looks cool, not fake or acid wash or anything. It looked like it needed something, so we bought a Metallica patch at the mall and Jennifer sewed it on.

At 3:55 PM I'm walking up the drive to the band house. The lawn hasn't been mowed in a long time. There are dandelions growing everywhere, and part of an old picket fence is rotting in the middle of the yard. I'm still not

sure whose house it is. I figured Grant
lives here, but who knows.

Grant's still the only guy in the band
who's friendly to me, although he's
actually not all that nice. Not to anyone,
really. While I'm plugging in, the
drummer stares at me the whole time.

"Hey, look! Duncan's wearing a new
widdle jacket," he says. The other guys
barely even look up.

"Nice jacket, kid. Metallica. How
cool. Do you even know who Metallica
is?" says the drummer.

There's a dipping feeling in my
stomach. I always get nervous if someone's putting me down in front of
other people. Don't say anything, I tell
myself. Just ignore it.

"Hey, idiot. You hear me? Are you
deaf or what?" says the drummer.

Jesus. I freeze up. What's with this
guy, anyway? I hate this.

"Hey, Larry. Shut up. Don't be a jerk," says Grant.

Larry shuts up, but he doesn't look happy. Grant's the leader in this group. Even though I'm freaked out by the weird vibe, I'm happy that Grant stands up for me. Maybe he's not such a bad guy.

Unbelievably, the practice goes really, really well. Larry may hate me, but we're clicking in pretty great as a rhythm section. The bass and the drums sort of lock in, like a unit. It's so loud though. I'd really like to wear earplugs, but when I try using some for the second practice, the guys all say I'm a wuss. Too bad they are those bright red industrial ones. Maybe they wouldn't notice otherwise.

After a couple of hours, we hang it up.

"Listen, you guys," says Grant. "I got us a gig. It's a house party, over in Tillicum. It's next Saturday. You guys good for that?"

"Right on. Nice work, Grant," says the drummer.

Man, I'm excited. This'll be my first gig with a real live rock band. And it should be a cool party too, I bet. To tell you the truth, I haven't been to too many parties. Except for ones with Jason and the guys. And they're not even real parties. There's no girls, for starters. And we mostly play stupid board games—like Risk—or watch dumb comedy movies. No liquor or anything.

As I put my bass into the case, it comes to me. I can ask Jennifer to the party. That'll be cool. Really, really cool. Man, things are going good after all.

Grant and I walk out together to the sidewalk. He tells me my bass playing is improving and not to worry about the drummer being a dick and all. I'm feeling good, like I really fit in for a change. A car horn honks. I look up and see Jason and his mom in her Range Rover.

"Hey, buddy. Warp drive, warp drive!" says Jason. He's smiling and all hyper and everything. "You dudes need a ride?"

Jason's wearing a Bart Simpson T-shirt. He actually looks a little like Bart—same sticking-up hairdo, same goofy smile.

"You know this doof?" says Grant. Loudly. He sounds like Larry the drummer.

"Uh…no. I mean. Not really. Some kid from school. He follows me around, like," I say. Softly, so that Jason won't hear.

I'm not even looking at Jason and his mom. Jason calls out again, but I can't really make it out. Grant and I keep walking toward my bus stop. Then I hear the Range Rover drive away.

Grant's talking about a new metal band I should really check out. He wants to burn me a copy of their CD. But I don't really take it in. My ears are hot. I wish Grant would stop talking. When the bus finally comes, I'm glad. I sit in the back with my bass leaning in the corner. All those good feelings from rehearsal— hearing about the party gig and Grant sticking up for me—have disappeared. I feel kind of sick.

As soon as I get home, I phone Jason.

"Hey, bud," I say when he answers. There's just silence on his end. But Jason's there. I can tell from his breathing.

"Hey…Sorry about not talking to you on the street earlier on. Grant and

I were discussing some, like, band business. I only saw it was you and your mom after you left."

Jason sighs. "How could you tell it was me and Mom if we'd already left?"

That's Jason for you. Mr. Logical. He's like Spock sometimes. Usually this pisses me off, but this time I'm just glad he's talking.

"Yeah. Hey, I'm sorry."

"You and this band. You've changed, you know that? Like you're too cool now to hang around with me and the guys. You remember the guys? Your friends?"

Jason sounds really mad. I've never heard him like this before.

"You and that stupid jean jacket. You look like a real jerk. A real poser, you know," he says.

This actually makes me mad. I really hate it when people criticize the way I look or the way I act. I can feel myself getting choked. I'm about to let Jason have it. Then I remember ignoring him on the street. He's my best friend. Maybe I am a jerk.

"Jason, I'm sorry. I guess I did see you on the street. I didn't know how to act. But anyway. Hey, do you want to come to a party?"

Silence on the line. Then Jason says, suspiciously, "What party?"

I tell him about the party in Tillicum, and how the band's going to play and how I'm going to invite Jennifer. And that he can come too. After a while, Jason warms up and he gets all excited—he's back to being the old Jason. That's what I like about him. He never holds a grudge for very long. Not like me. When I get mad, it can last for a long time.

Then Dad phones to say he and Terry are going to have dinner out, and for me to fix my own. This kind of burns me, but then I remember acting like a jerk to Jason. For some reason that makes me feel better. My emotions are on a teeter-totter. I microwave a TV dinner—frozen lasagna. And then I snag one of Dad's beers out of the fridge.

He's gonna kill me later, but hey… it's been a rough day, right? Right.

Chapter Seven

Sundays are usually boring for me. The dull day of the weekend. Saturdays mean shopping or hanging out or maybe going to a movie. Sundays are like a flat tire. Homework. Mope around. Dad says it's just me. It's more about my mental attitude. But I still think Sundays are pretty lame.

But this Sunday's different. It's the day Terry said she's taking me to meet her brother. The guy who plays the organ. Who was in a professional band. Terry did say that he was kind of strange. Maybe he's a weirdo. But still, I'm excited.

Terry picks me up in the afternoon. Her car's a beater—a 1984 Toyota with shiny gray duct tape to keep the back taillight from falling off. Dad would never let that happen to his car. But then, he's got a brand new BMW. So it's not like the taillight's going to fall off or anything.

On the way over, Terry talks about her brother, Houston. She tells me stories about when they were little kids. He was a real joker, sounds like. One time he invited her up into his tree house and then nailed the door shut. Terry was stuck in the tree house yelling for hours. When he finally pried open the door, she was crying. It sounds pretty mean. But I've never had a sister or a brother. Maybe that's normal. And she's laughing when she tells the story.

When we pull up to Houston's house, my heart sinks. It's an old one that at one time was probably really nice. Like back in 1900 or something. There's a big front porch with fancy columns. But the whole thing is sagging in the middle. So is the roof. And the paint's peeling off.

The grass is three feet high, which makes me wonder if maybe musicians just aren't good with gardening. And there's a rusted baby buggy in the middle of the lawn. Weird. If this was my house, I'd get rid of the buggy, for starters.

The door's got a big metal knocker in the shape of a lion's head. Terry knocks—*whack, whack, whack*—and then she knocks again. Still no answer. She walks over to a window, looks in, bobbing her head around, trying to see in. Terry looks at me and makes a face as if to say, "What the heck?" Then she knocks again.

Finally the door creaks open. The guy who opens it is wearing a stained white underwear shirt. You know, the type they call a "wife-beater"? He's in sweatpants. His hair is long and tousled and gray. He has a five-day growth of beard. And he looks a lot like Terry. That is, if Terry were a guy and hadn't taken a shower in two years.

"Hey, man," he says, rubbing his scrubby jaw. "What's up?"

"Houston. Houston, this is Duncan. You know, the young man I told you about? The musician. I said we were going to come this afternoon. You didn't forget, did you?"

"Forget?" Houston sticks his hand down the waistband of his sweats and readjusts something. "Naw. I knew you guys were comin'. I just…ah. Well, come on in."

It's dark and just plain strange in Houston's living room. He pulls back the ratty curtains, letting a little light on the situation. Holy cow! I mean, I'm not the neatest guy in the world. But this place is a total dump. Magazines and newspapers strewn all over the place. Beer cans on the coffee table. Piles of empty pizza and KFC boxes. The place is dusty and full of mothballs. Really dirty. It smells like dead mice.

"Oh, Houston. I thought you were going to hire a cleaning lady to help you with all this," says Terry. She scoops up an armful of magazines and sets them down in a neat pile. Clouds of dust puff up.

"Oh yeah. Sure. I mean to do that real soon. It's, like, on my list." Houston winks at me. I don't wink back. He's freaking me out a little, to tell the truth.

Not knowing what to do, I walk over to look at some posters on the wall. One says, *The Amazing Rhythm Kings— Live at the Yale*. Another says, *At the Triple Door for Two Nights Only!—The Amazing Rhythm Kings*.

"That was my band, Duncan," Houston says. "The Rhythm Kings. Pure, one-hundred-percent southern-fried soul. Only we weren't from the South. We were from Victoria, British Columbia, the land of tweed raincoats and tea-bag earrings."

Houston starts laughing, a funny kind of hoarse laugh. A smoker's laugh. I was happy he remembered my name.

In a corner of the living room was a piano. Or I thought it was. But when I got closer, I saw it had two sets of keys.

"Is this an organ?" I ask.

"It sure enough is," says Houston. He slides over onto the bench and flicks a switch. There's a whirring noise. Kind of like starting a car.

"This, my friend, is a 1969 Hammond B-3 organ. The king of the rock and jazz organs. The king of all organs. And over there—the big thing that looks like a wooden fridge? That's a genuine Leslie 122 speaker."

Houston bends over the organ and starts playing. And let me tell you. I think my life changed from that point on.

This thing sounded…well, indescribable. The sound filled the room, a giant swirling thing. Almost like a gigantic human voice. Houston cranked it up so loud, you could see dust rise from the mantel over the fireplace. He kept pulling little switches in and out, here and there. Sometimes it sounded glassy and smooth, sometimes it sounded down-and-dirty greasy. Sometimes it whispered, sometimes it shrieked and moaned like a crazy witch or a monster. It was something else.

And this guy is crazy good on the keyboards. His sound is so funky and just plain fantastic. Let me tell you, I went from thinking he was a doofus in a dirty undershirt to believing Houston was the coolest dude on planet Earth.

"Holy crap," I say when he's finished.

"Duncan!" says Terry.

"That's okay. This young brother's just responding righteously to the sound o' the mighty B-3," says Houston, pretending to sound like a black guy. Then he bends over and coughs. "Wanna try?"

Did I? Yes! But I'm a little nervous too. I mean, I took piano lessons when I was a kid. For six years, in fact. But the organ was a whole new deal.

I sit beside Houston on the bench. He shows me the on/off lever that makes the horn speakers in the Leslie speaker whirl around. He shows me how those switches—they're called drawbars—push in and out to change the sound. After about thirty minutes or so, I'm sort of getting the hang of it. Houston shows me how to play a few blues licks that sound really amazing.

"Know this one?" he says. And then he starts to play "Green Onions." Only when Houston plays it, it sounds different. Of course there's no drums, no band. But the sound is just, well…huge. Massive. I'm so excited I could jump up and do some kind of crazy leprechaun dance around the living room. But I don't, because that would make me look like a complete numbnut.

We goof around on that organ for a couple of hours. Or more. The time just flies by. In fact, I don't notice Terry has even left until there is a knock on the door. It's Terry. She's brought a whole load of Chinese food. I eat like a starving man. Two and half platefuls.

"How did you like that?" Terry asks me in her car on the way home.

"Terrific. I love Chinese food."

"No, silly. I mean playing the organ," she says.

"I loved it," I say. "Houston's great. He's cool, you know."

Terry looks ahead, tapping her fingers on the steering wheel. "He's had a tough time of it," she says.

"What do you mean?" I ask.

"Well, I told you how he got all caught up in his band before. It was too much for him. I think he had a nervous breakdown."

"You mean he went nuts or something?" I ask.

"It's like when the world gets too much for a person. They sort of go off the deep end, maybe shut down," she says. "Houston gave up. He hasn't tried to get back into music ever since then. It's been a couple of years. And he's sort of a recluse."

"He doesn't leave the house and all that?"

"Yeah. Well, he'll go out for groceries. That's about it. His friends used to come around, but that dried up. I'm worried about him."

I look over at Terry. She looks like she's going to cry. I don't know what to say, so I just stare out the window, keeping quiet. It starts to rain a little. Just spatters. And then it begins to come down hard.

Chapter Eight

I'm trying a little harder in school, catching up on overdue assignments and stuff. You know why? Houston. It's weird, but I keep thinking about the guy. He's a great musician and all, but if Terry's right, it seems like he's burned himself out. I've got it in my mind, that could happen to me too. You know, becoming a lonely old musician in a creepy old house with a rusty baby buggy rotting away on the front lawn. It freaks me out. So I'm putting in some real grunt work—probably the hardest I've worked at school since Mom died.

It's extra tough hanging in at school, because all week I'm thinking about the party on Saturday night. It's the band's first gig, so it's a big deal. I asked Jennifer to come, and right away she said yes. She seemed happy. It's going pretty well between us. She's the first girlfriend I've ever had. I mean, I think she's my girlfriend. And Jason's coming too.

To get ready for the gig, the band is practicing three times this week: Monday, Wednesday and Thursday. Primal Thunk is getting tight. Me and the drummer are really locking in well, sounding like a unit. Like a machine. The music is all fast metal: *thunka-thunka-thunka-thunk*. I'm not sure if metal's my favorite thing, but it's fun to play in a band. It's a rush, you know. I can't compare it to anything. Maybe it's like white-water rafting, when a crew of your buddies zooms down the rushing river, all paddling together. I don't know. I've never done that. But that's how it feels.

We're supposed to get to the party house at 8:00 on Saturday night to set up our gear. *Set up our gear*. I like the sound of that—kind of professional.

Saturday finally rolls around. Dad and I have supper together. And right off, between bites of Shake'n Bake chicken and mashed potato, he starts lecturing me about the party.

"Duncan, exactly what kind of gathering is this going to be?" he says.

"I dunno," I say, spearing a piece of broccoli with my fork. "A party-party."

"Don't get fresh with me. You know, if I don't like the sound of this, you can just stay at home."

Dad's frowning. Jesus.

"It's just a regular party. With regular people. And my band's going to play at it. Jennifer's coming. So's Jason."

He doesn't say anything, like he's mulling it over. I know Dad's thinking if Jason's there, it's probably okay. He likes Jason because he's a good student. Also, Dad's met Jennifer and he likes her too. He said she's polite and doesn't wear too much makeup. Which I guess is true.

"Well," he says after a moment, "just be careful. No drinking."

"Okay," I say.

"And no drugs."

I mumble under my breath.

"What was that?" says Dad.

"Nothing."

After dinner I run upstairs to dress for the party. I'm going to wear my rocker jean jacket. I ripped off that stupid Metallica patch after the drummer bugged me about it. No big deal. Heck, I don't even like Metallica.

Looking at myself in the mirror, I wonder if I even look like a guy in a rock band. My hair's still pretty short. And my face is kinda young-looking. My cheeks are all rosy and healthy-like. Crap. I muss up my hair so it's all jagged. Better, I guess. Can't tell.

I grab my bass and head downstairs. Terry's come by—she's sitting on the couch with Dad. They're watching some stupid animal show on TV. It's about all these little pathetic-looking turtles making a beeline down the beach and then swimming in the waves.

"Hey, you," says Terry. "Going somewhere?"

"It's our first gig. You know, Primal Thunk." I grin. It sounds cool to say that.

Dad looks over at me.

"Duncan, go comb your hair. You look like you just rolled out of bed," he says.

I put my hand to my hair. It's all stiff and spiky because I put gel on to keep it in place.

"Dad, it's supposed to look like this."

"Duncan. I'm not kidding. You look like a mess. You go upstairs and comb your hair."

"No," I say.

There's a silence of, like, five seconds. It's a funny thing, but five seconds seems like an awfully long time when people are mad at each other and all. It seems like five hours. I've never said no to Dad before. Not directly. There are butterflies in my stomach.

"Oh, hon, let him go. That's how kids wear their hair these days," says Terry finally.

Uh-oh. Dad hates it when anyone contradicts him like that. Now I've gone from butterflies to feeling scared.

"Terry," says Dad, not looking at her. "Please be quiet. I'm trying to set boundaries for my son."

Terry's face kind of changes. I wish Dad hadn't said that to her.

"Go—comb—your—hair," he says to me again.

"No," I say. And I grab my bass and walk out the front door. On the sidewalk I wait for Jason. His mom's giving me and Jennifer a ride to the party. The wind's cold, even icy, but that's okay because my face is all hot now, like someone slapped me. I keep thinking Dad's going to come out and make me stay home. But he doesn't. Loud voices are coming from our house. I feel awful and wish none of the last ten minutes had happened.

I see headlights, and a Range Rover pulls up. It's Jason, his mom and Jennifer.

I throw my gear in the back, tumble in and feel in my pocket for the address, scribbled on a piece of paper. The tricky thing is, I want Jason's mom to drop us off a block away, rather than right at the door. That way no one will know we don't drive, and that one of our moms had to give us a ride. So it won't look so lame and all.

"You can drop us off here, Mrs. Richmond," I say. "Thanks for the ride. Appreciate it."

"That's not the address," says Jason.

"Shut up," I whisper. "We can't let your mom drop us off right at the front door. We'll look like total dorks."

Jason gives me a dirty look. "Oh, man," he hisses. "Not this stuff again. It's like you're ashamed of us or something."

"No, I'm not," I say. "It's just…oh, just shut up, Jason, for Christ's sake."

Jason is pissed. Jennifer looks at us both, sighs a little sigh, but doesn't say anything. I don't know if she overheard. It's hard to read her face. She's all dressed up for the party, in a black dress that's kind of glittery. She looks really awesome, if you want to know the truth. I can't believe she's going to a real party with me.

We walk up the block. The wind is like ice needles. I shiver in my jean jacket. Jennifer doesn't even have a jacket on—maybe it was a stupid idea to get dropped off so far away. I offer her my jacket, but she says no. It's dark now, and the street numbers are hard to make out. It's a pretty crummy area. The kind of street where people park their stupid big-wheel pickups in the middle of their chewed-up front lawns.

Some guys wearing hoodies suddenly run in our direction. They brush by, and one bumps my bass guitar case.

"Hey, watch it man," I say without thinking.

He stops, turns slowly around and walks back to us. I feel my stomach fall. Oh crap. What now?

"What's your problem, kid?" he says. He's about twenty, with a face full of pimples and a homemade tattoo of a cross on his neck.

"No problem. Sorry. You just, you know...you knocked into my guitar case."

The guy just keeps staring at me, like he hates me or something. Then one of his friends shouts out, "Hey, Pig-man, come on. We're gonna be late!"

Pig-man looks over his shoulder at his friend, then back at me. He says,

"Just watch it, punk." And then he takes off.

"Jesus," says Jason. Jennifer takes my arm and shivers a big body shiver. Is she cold or scared? I look at the number of the house in front of us. This is it.

Oh god.

This place makes Houston's house and the Primal Thunk practice space look like Donald Trump's mansion. There are motorbikes parked in the front yard with guys sitting on them, drinking beer. Some I recognize, but I'm not sure. Some of them look older, like in their twenties. The front door of the house is open, and there's loud thumping rock music coming out.

A girl in a purple tank top stumbles up the front path toward us.

"Are you Tom?" she said, grabbing my arm. "Tommy? Are you Tom?"

Yikes. She sinks down at our feet, all crumpled. She has dyed blond hair with black roots. The guys sitting on the motorbikes start laughing at her. I kneel beside her. I don't know what to do, so I hold her hand, which feels clammy. She seems okay though. I mean, she's breathing and everything. Just passed out. I help her into a lawn chair near the front door.

"Duncan?" says Jennifer. Her face looks scared.

"Don't worry guys," I say. "Everything's cool. Let's go in."

I'm trying to act confident, but to be honest, I feel scared. What kind of a party is this, anyway? Who are these biker guys?

The place is stuffed with people. We have to squeeze by to get through the front hall. I think I recognize some kids from high school, but no one I've ever talked to before.

The living room is crowded too. It smells funny, like rancid milk.

The stereo's so loud you can't talk—it's a punk song, with the singer screaming "Everybody gonna die now!" over and over. If this was a movie or a TV show, I'd laugh. But it's not.

I look at Jennifer and instantly regret bringing her to something like this. Her shoulders are hunched up like she doesn't want anyone here to touch her. Her body language says, "Get me out of here." Jason looks at me and opens his eyes wide, as if to say, "What the heck?"

"Hey, who's this douche?" says a ratty-looking short guy in a flannel shirt. "Did your momma dress you, boy?"

He's talking to Jason. Jason is dressed kind of weird, especially for someone going to a party. He has a short-sleeved shirt on, buttoned right to the neck. The shirt's pattern is old-fashioned cars. And he's wearing a pair of khakis. It looks like he should be manning the sugar-cookie booth at a church fair.

"Who invited this jerk to the party?" says the ratty guy. He blows smoke from his cigarette in Jason's face, like some actor from a gangster movie.

Jason coughs. "Smoking will kill you," he says.

"What?" Ratty moves toward Jason a little, sticking out his chin like he wants to fight.

"Jason." I yell it into his ear, because someone's cranked up that stupid punk song even louder. "Don't even talk to him."

At that moment, Jennifer kind of starts and lets out a little yip. I look over, and Ratty jumps back. He's grinning. I just know he's groped her or something like that.

"Hey, dude, you made it!" It's Grant, holding out his hand and smiling like he's Hugh Hefner at the Playboy mansion. He seems different, like he's blurry or something. Maybe it's just me. This is turning out to be one very weird night.

"This your woman?" he says, pointing at Jennifer with his beer. He ignores Jason.

"This is Jennifer," I say. She smiles and holds out her hand, even though she was probably groped five seconds ago. Jennifer's always nice to people. Maybe this party will work out after all. Grant smiles again and nods.

The band already brought all the gear over, including the bass amp, so I don't have much to set up. I was hoping we'd have more time before Primal Thunk played, just so Jason, Jennifer and I could hang out a little. But Grant looks at his watch, burps and says, "Okay, 9:00 PM. We're supposed to... we're supposed to play now. So let's get started, boys."

The drummer clicks his sticks four times over his head, and we're off. The music's really rehearsed, I've gotta admit. But it's like the volume is way louder than we usually play it. I must have missed the meeting where everyone agreed we'd crank the volume up to eleven. After the first tune, I rip the corner off my set list and make a set of earplugs with the rolled-up paper.

Still, it's going over pretty well. I can't see Jennifer or Jason. The floor in front of us is full of people dancing. A good sign. Actually, they're just jumping up and down. Mostly guys—including some of the biker dudes. A superhairy no-shirt guy is standing right in front of me, flailing his head from side to side. He's got this really long hair and a ZZ Top beard, so it looks pretty incredible. Sometimes I can feel his hair, which is wet and sweaty, slap across my right hand. Which is kind of disgusting.

After three tunes, Grant comes over.

"You're playing good, Dunc," he says. "Want some Jack?"

He takes a bottle of Jack Daniels whiskey from his back pocket. The drummer's looking at me, smirking. So I grab the bottle and take a slug. It tastes horrible, like liquid fire. But Grant's looking at me, grinning in an "I dare you" kind of way. So I take another big slug.

"Rock and roll, my brother," he says. "I always thought you were kind of a pussy."

Grant pats me on the back. Him calling me *brother* makes me feel good. There's no time to think about this though, because right away we're into another song. And then another. And then in no time, our set is done. I look at the crowd, expecting applause or something. The funny thing, no one even claps. Except for this hairy guy.

He goes crazy, smacking his hands together and whooping, like he's front row at a U2 concert. I make a mental note to avoid him, in case he's a psycho.

"We'll be right back after a short break and a cold beer," Grant mumbles into the microphone. He reaches behind the drum kit and starts handing out cans of beer to the band. The can is cold in my hand. This feels good, because my hand is sort of numb from hitting the strings so hard. But I don't really want it.

"No thanks," I say. That whiskey is already hitting me. I feel light-headed. It's really noisy in the room—the stereo's back on, and someone in the corner is yelling. Something about the money some guy called Jack owes him. He sounds pissed.

"Hey, McCann. I thought you weren't a total weenie," Grant says. "My mistake."

So I grab the stupid can of beer and take a long swig. It actually feels good going down my throat, it's so hot in the room. Grant hands me the bottle of Jack again. I take a long pull, then drink some more beer.

"That's more like it, dude. Now you're rocking," says Grant.

There's a tap on my arm. It's Jason and Jennifer.

"Hey, stranger," says Jennifer.

"Hi. Where were you guys?"

"We took a little walk outside. Some of those motorbike guys are making a bonfire in the front yard. In an oil drum," says Jason.

I look at Jennifer in her party dress. I get that sinking feeling again.

"How'd you guys like our set?" says Grant, who's staring at Jennifer in a way I don't like.

"Well, we were outside, but it sounded great. Actually, I was wondering if I could ask you something," says Jason.

Oh god. Don't say it, Jason. Don't say it. Please.

"Yeah, I was wondering if we could use your music. Me and Dunc are making a movie. It could be, like, the soundtrack."

"What kind of movie?" says Grant.

"It's a remake of *Raiders of the Lost Ark*. We've been making it since we were twelve. It's really cool." Jason goes on to give Grant all the superdorky details, talking fast and breathlessly like he always does when he's excited. I'm embarrassed, but at the same time, I'm getting this weird floating feeling from the booze.

After Jason finishes explaining about the movie, no one speaks for a few seconds.

"Oh, man, that's so lame," says Grant, finally. "You guys sound like a bunch of babies. What are you, in grade two?"

Jason looks at Grant open-mouthed, like someone just punched him in the face. Then, without saying a word, he turns and walks out the front door. Jason has officially left the party.

Meanwhile, Grant's wandered off somewhere. I think maybe I should go after Jason, but my legs feel kinda wobbly. It's like my body's wrapped in cotton.

"Duncan, maybe we should go home now," says Jennifer.

I'd forgotten she was still here. Maybe I'm drunk.

"No…it's cool. Beside, I have to, uh…play another set."

"Please. I think I should go home."

Suddenly, I feel drunk. At least, I think so. The room is starting to spin a little.

"Aw, come on, Jen," I say, thinking we should take this boyfriend-girlfriend thing to the next stage. "Lemme have… I mean, how about a kiss?"

I turn to hug Jennifer, but stumble. Then something terrible happens. Both my hands land on her chest. One of the straps on her dress snaps. Jennifer's face sort of crumbles. Then, without saying another word, she runs out the door, one hand holding the broken strap. Oh no. What have I done?

"Your bitch leave?" says Grant, who like magic is somehow back at my elbow again.

"Yeah," I say, slurring. So really, it comes out like "Yeshh."

"Who cares," he says. "Come on, let's play."

We play another set, but it's nowhere near as good as the first. It's horrible in fact. After every couple of songs Grant gives me a beer and another shot of whisky. I go along with it—hey, I'm a rocker now, right?

After that…well, it's hard to explain what happened. Even today I can't quite figure it out. First I'm playing music with the band. And the next thing I remember, I'm waking in total darkness. I guess I passed out. I can hardly breathe. A CD player is on in some other room, skipping on the same two notes over and over. But aside from that, it's quiet.

I try to move, but it's hard to shift my shoulders. Stuck. I struggle, then finally get free. Somehow, I got wedged behind this old, dirty, smelly couch. Unbelievable. Not only that, but I've been sick on myself, like all down the front of my pants. And I feel really, really horrible, like I'm gonna die or something.

The digital clock in the room—
the only light—says it's 5:14. Oh no.
Dad's gonna kill me. So I decide to
phone Terry. Her phone number's still
in my wallet from the time we visited
Houston.

Terry sounds groggy on the phone,
but amazingly, she's cool and agrees to
pick me up. Thank god I still have the
address on that piece of paper so I can
tell her where I am. I wait on the street
holding my bass. Couldn't even find
the case. My head is pounding. At least
I wiped the sick off my pants with a
dirty towel from the kitchen. I feel
like lying down on the sidewalk. Terry
raises her eyebrows when she sees the
condition I'm in, but doesn't say a word
other than, "Jump in."

The next thing I know, I'm waking
up in Terry's apartment, on her couch.
The clock on the wall says 12:34 PM.

My jeans are washed and folded on the coffee table. I walk over to the sink, drink a glass of water...and throw up into the sink. What a start to the day.

Chapter Nine

If you think Dad was mad when I finally made it home that day, you're exactly right.

I'd say on a scale of ten, it was... oh, maybe about a fourteen. Or a fifteen. Dad lectured me for about an hour. It was extra rough because my head ached—in fact, my whole body did.

I just felt like going to bed, which is what I did after Dad was done.

For the last four weeks, I've been on the straight and narrow. It's been go to school, come home, do my chores, listen to Dad lecture me on the evils of drinking, and go to bed early.

Me and Dad drove back to the party house the day after to try to get my bass case back. That really hairy dude answered, but when Dad explained what we wanted, Mr. Hairy just said, "I've never seen this damned kid before in my life," and slammed the door. So that was that. Although Dad was pretty choked.

Maybe it's not that big of a deal about the case anyway. I'm not really playing bass anymore. Dad made me quit the band after the party. He says those guys are a bad influence. Maybe they are. I don't know. It was pretty fun playing the music. But I can't really say they were my friends.

Anyhow, something better happened. I started hanging out a lot at Houston's, playing his Hammond B-3 organ. Dad said that was okay. And Houston says I can play any time I want. And guess what? I've started to get really good on the organ. No kidding. Much better than I was on bass. Houston says it's because every musician has only one instrument that comes naturally to them. For me, it's the Hammond B-3. Love the grinding, whirling sound. It just sounds fantastic to me.

Jason was mad at me after the party. Not sure why, since it was Grant who made fun of the dumb movie project, not me. But now we're good buddies again because of something that happened in the school cafeteria. Jason and I were eating lunch when Grant came by. We hadn't talked since I told him I was quitting Primal Thunk. He'd just said "whatever" on the phone and hung up.

Anyway, so Grant sees us and says, "Hey, babies. How's your widdle movie show coming along? What is it again, *Raiders of the Lost Tinkerbell*?"

"Shut up, Grant," I say.

"Shut up, yourself. You lightweight. You and your baby-ass friend."

"He's a lot smarter than you."

I thought Grant was going to hit me. I really did. His face went all funny, like he was thinking four or five things all at once. But instead of slugging me, he just paused for a second, then kept walking. Jason didn't say anything about it, but I could tell he was happy because I stood up for him in public. He bought me some French fries right after that. And Jason is usually pretty cheap.

It didn't go so well with Jennifer after that party though. I mean, I apologized to her and she seemed okay with that, but when I asked her out afterward— two times to go for coffee, and one time to a movie—she always had an excuse. Once she said she has to visit her grandmother, which I think is code for *Get lost, pal*. Then yesterday I saw her in the hallway, holding hands with some guy from the basketball team. Too bad.

It's funny, but Dad and I have started to get along better now than ever, even though he's still being really strict. He said we need to spend more time together, like "father and son" time. At first it was awkward. We'd go to a movie or even fly fishing one time. I felt like he was just feeling sorry for me or something. Just going through the motions, like following the Rulebook for Good Fathers Whose Sons Get Wasted at Parties. But after a while, things did get easier and smoother between us. I can't explain it, exactly. It's kind of cool though.

The weird thing is, Dad broke up with Terry about the same time Jennifer and I stopped going out. I asked Terry about it—I still see her all the time at Houston's house. She says my dad's a good guy and all, but their personalities are just too different.

"Dad's too uptight," I said.

"No, Duncan. Don't say that. Your father is a good man. He's a great dad, and he cares about you a lot. I know that. We're just different personalities."

Terry smiled, and the corners of her eyes wrinkled. For an adult, she's pretty cool.

It's a drag not to have a girlfriend anymore. But there's another girl in the school band, Carrie, who I kind of like. She's new—she moved here from Edmonton. And guess what? She plays the drums. Carrie's pretty good. I'm thinking of asking her to join my band.

Oh yeah, that's right. I have my own band now. How cool is that?

We're rehearsing at Houston's house. And guess what? Jason's playing my old bass. He's not that good, in fact, he's pretty bad. And it doesn't help that there's a crack in the neck of the bass—it somehow happened the night of the party. The bass goes out of tune a lot now. But he's learning pretty fast. Of course, I'm playing organ. And we also have a guitarist—a guy who answered the ad I posted online. He's really, really good.

Houston sometimes sits in with the band on organ. When that happens, I just hunker down on the couch and watch. I'm happy to do it. He's so good, and you can learn stuff if you concentrate real hard. He taught me how to play "Green Onions"—maybe not quite as good as him, but pretty well—and now the whole band's learning it.

Yeah, I'm definitely going to ask Carrie to join the band. That'll be cool.

By the way, we need a name for the band. You got any ideas? I'd be open to hearing your suggestions, my friend. As long as they're not too lame-ass or anything.

Kidding. Just kidding.

Adrian Chamberlain has always wanted to be a rock star. While holding down a day job as an entertainment writer for the Victoria *Times Colonist*, he indulges his fantasies (albeit on a reduced scale) by playing organ and piano for The Soul Shakers, a Victoria rhythm-and-blues band.

orca soundings

The following is an excerpt from
another exciting Orca Soundings novel,
Reaction by Lesley Choyce.

978-1-55469-277-4 $9.95 pb
978-1-55469-278-1 $16.95 lib

ZACH AND ASHLEY HAVE BEEN GOING
out for a while, and things are going well—until
Ashley finds out she is pregnant. She is angry and
blames Zach. She wouldn't be in this state if he
hadn't tried to take their relationship further than
she wanted. Insistent at first on an abortion, she
turns against Zach. Confused, Zach struggles with
what he should do and what his responsibilities
are. Coming to terms with the reactions of their
families and friends, Zach realizes that this is a
decision that he and Ashley must make together.

Chapter One

"Zach, I'm pregnant."

Ashley dropped the bombshell on me between classes at school. I remember the exact time, because I was standing in front of the hallway clock. 11:11. Yep. Eleven eleven in the morning. It was a Tuesday.

She was looking straight at me when she blurted it right out.

"That's impossible," I snapped back. And I looked away from her and back to the stupid clock. The time changed to 11:12.

"It's true," she said. And then she began to cry.

I put my arm around her and pulled her toward me. "Let's go," I said.

"Where?"

"Anywhere. Let's get out of here."

I led her down the hall and out the front door into the bright sunlight. As I opened the door of the school, I had this feeling that maybe nothing in my life would ever be the same again.

That was exactly how it happened. I will never forget the feeling. I had never been more scared in my life. Never. I know that I wasn't the first guy to hear those words from his girlfriend, but it felt that way. Sad to say, I wasn't even thinking about Ashley at the time. I was thinking about me. What was I going to do? What was going to happen to me? What would this do to my life?

We walked for almost an hour. Neither of us talked at first. Then I began to rationalize, and one part of my brain wanted to convince us both that it must be some kind of mistake.

"Are you sure?" I asked.

"Yes."

"How sure?"

"Very sure."

"Maybe you made a mistake."

"Maybe *we* made a mistake," she said.

"I mean, about the tests. Did you buy one of those testing things from the drugstore?"

"Three of them."

"Maybe they were defective."

"They were three different brands. They all had the same results."

I was still looking for a way out of this. I was looking for a way to get *me* out of this. I almost asked her if she was sure it was me, that I was the father. But I didn't.

Because just then I remembered. Two months ago. We'd been partying. (That's what we did, Ashley and I. We partied big-time.) We'd been drinking. And my parents were gone for the weekend. And one thing led to another. And we were so into it.

And I knew the condom broke, but I didn't mention a word to her. Hey, I thought it would wreck the mood. Plus, what were the chances?

So there I was, sixteen years old, walking through the suburban streets with my fifteen-year-old girlfriend who has just told me she's pregnant. And I'm still thinking, this can't be happening to me.

"I'm scared," Ashley said, leaning into me and holding tightly onto my arm.

I didn't tell her how scared I was, and I didn't even tell her about the condom then. I said what guys say in situations like this when the blood has drained out of their heads and they are screaming inside, panicking, ready to run for the hills and never come back. I said, "Everything is going to be all right."

orca soundings

For more information on all the books
in the Orca Soundings series, please visit
www.orcabook.com.